Toddler: paused.

Written by Lucy Janes

Illustrated by Elena Nikolaichuk

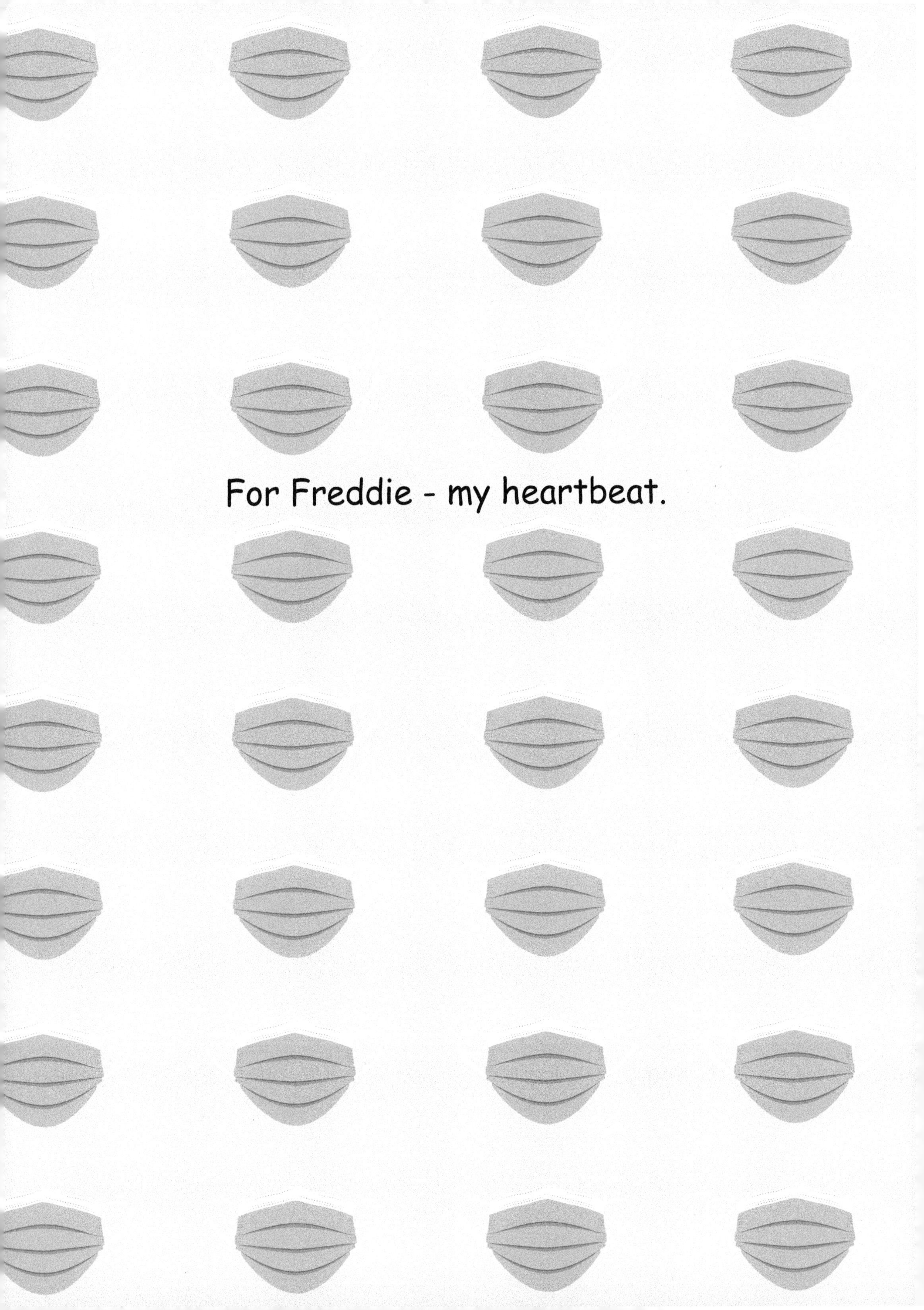

For Freddie - my heartbeat.

Days spent cuddling on the sofa in the coffee shop,
Meeting new mums and babies, chatter doesn't stop.

Trips to the supermarket, town or playground,
Looking, listening, people all around.

Exploring, learning, a whole, wide world to see.
Then one day... everything stopped!
How could this be?

he airport, the restaurants, the schools are all closed.
ow long for, nobody knows.

Watching the news for each day's update,
Wondering when we will be allowed our next playdate

Friends are no longer allowed to come round,
Life becomes repetitive, just waiting around.

Dad is working from home, taking over my play zone.

Weekends - locked down and curfews began,
From Saturday to Monday, staying home was the plan.

Every day's highlight was our walk in the fresh air,
No longer used to seeing people,
I'm trying hard not to stare.

Occasionally passing by someone we know,
A wave across the street is how we say hello.

Mask on! Keep your distance! Stay 6 feet apart!
Not seeing friends and family is breaking my heart.

PHARMACY +

Day after day after day after day,
Months pass by, all we can do is hope and pray.
Waiting to hear when the next date is easing,
Possible summer trips sound very pleasing.

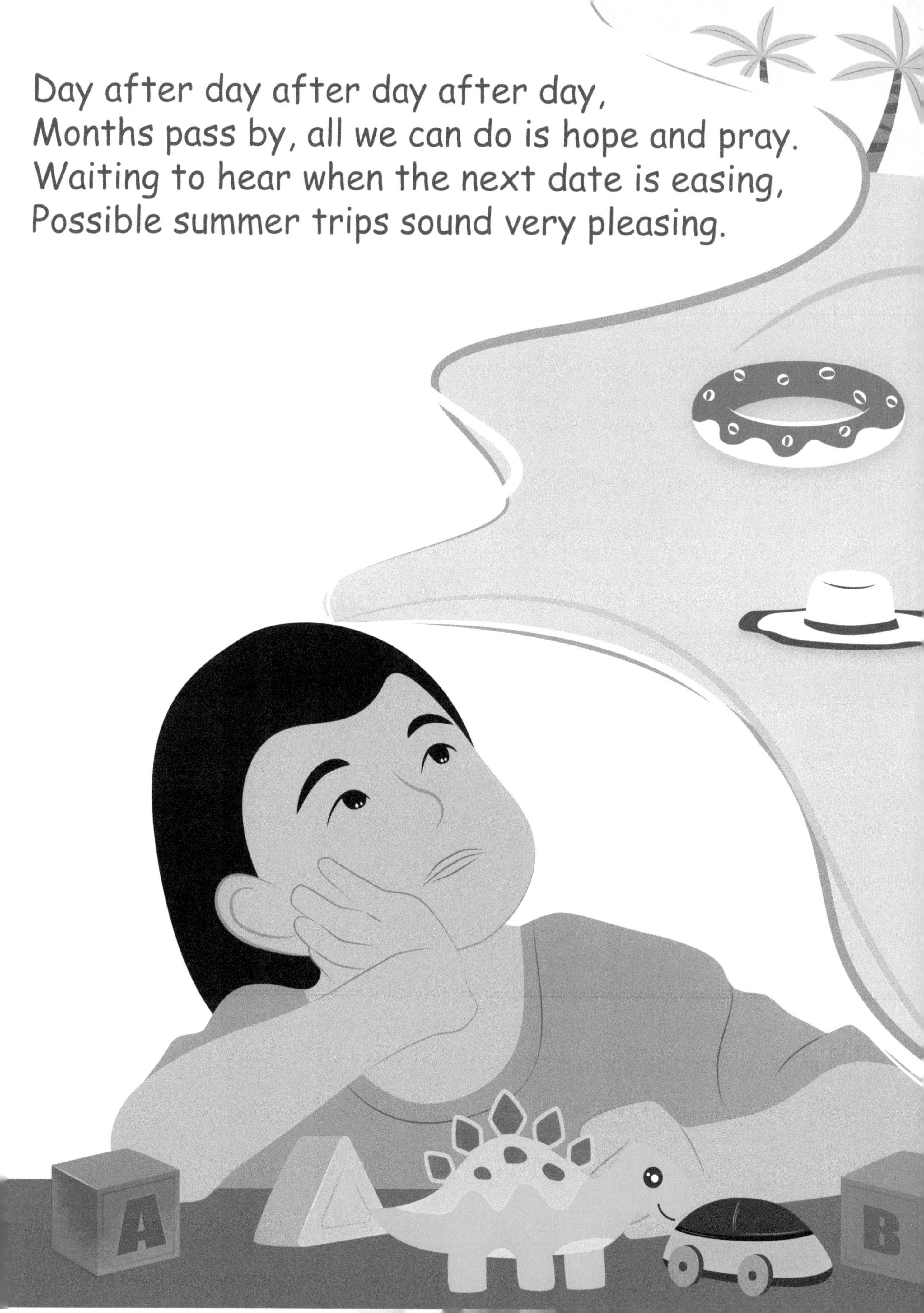

Hopefully not much longer,
We have worked hard together,
Learning what matters the most
Will stay with us forever.

Feeling nervous but being allowed out is so exciting,
We still have a long way to go and this virus, we will keep fighting.

What to do? Who to see? Where shall we go?
Please remember I'm still so little
and I need you to know,

I'm so used to not having people around,
It will take me time after being housebound.

In the big wide world, I will find my place,
Don't forget I'm still learning; this isn't a race.

A

ISBN: 978-1-9989969-0-2

Illustrator: Elena Nikolaichuk

Edition 1.

@toddlerpaused

toddlerpaused@gmail.com

Lightning Source UK Ltd.
Milton Keynes UK
UKHW050254200721
387415UK00006B/326